THE TREASURE TROOP

The Final Treasure

by Dori Hillestad Butler

illustrated by Tim Budgen

Penguin Workshop

For Bob—DHB

Thanks to Jay for all your hard work
and support—TB

PENGUIN WORKSHOP
An imprint of Penguin Random House LLC, New York

First published in the United States of America by Penguin Workshop,
an imprint of Penguin Random House LLC, New York, 2021

Visit us online at www.penguinrandomhouse.com.

Library of Congress Control Number: 2021019882

Book manufactured in Canada

ISBN 9780593094914 (pbk)
ISBN 9780593094921 (hc)

10 9 8 7 6 5 4 3 2 1 FRI
10 9 8 7 6 5 4 3 2 1 FRI

Chapter 1

CAPTAIN JOE RETURNS

Marly and her friends stood at the end of the Summer Island dock, waving eagerly as Captain Joe's boat zoomed toward them. It was eight o'clock in the morning, and they were heading home. But that wasn't why they were so excited.

"Do you have the spyglass?" Sai elbowed Marly.

"Right here." Marly held it up, then put it to her unpatched eye. She aimed the spyglass at the boat and adjusted the focus. Oh, wow! She

could actually see Captain Joe at the wheel! He wore a blue shirt and dark sunglasses, and his curly gray hair was blowing in the wind.

"Can I see?" Isla asked. Her cat ears headband cast a shadow over the water below them.

"Sure." Marly handed the spyglass to Isla and blinked a few times. But because she wore a patch over her good eye, everything remained out of focus. The patch was supposed to train her bad eye to work better, but while it was on her glasses, she had trouble seeing anything that wasn't right in front of her face. Ideally, she'd be able to stop wearing it soon.

"What do you think Captain Joe is going to give us?" Sai asked as he bounced from one foot to the other. The letter they'd found yesterday, written by Harry Summerling himself, told them to give the spyglass to Captain Joe, who would then give them something in return. But what? They'd already received a tree house and a trip to Summer Island.

"I hope it's information about where Harry's been all summer," Stella Lovelace said dryly. Stella was Harry Summerling's attorney. She was the one who'd brought Marly, Isla, and Sai to Summer Island. Until they'd read that letter, everyone, including Stella, believed Mr. Summerling drowned in a storm while searching for treasure a couple of months ago. But now they knew he was alive!

How can they go home without seeing or talking to him? Marly wondered. *Especially when he is probably close by!*

Isla passed the spyglass back to Marly and Marly pressed it to her eye again. "I wonder if Mr. Summerling is somewhere on that boat," she said. Captain Joe was getting close enough now that Marly had to back up to keep him in focus.

"Careful!" Stella put her hands out as Marly backed into her with a jolt.

"Oh, sorry," Marly said, righting herself.

"Ahoy there, Treasure Troop!" Captain Joe waved as he cut the motor and drifted toward the dock.

"Look what we have! Look what we have!" Sai jumped up and down. He couldn't wait until they were on the boat. "Show him, Marly!"

Marly held the spyglass above her head like it was a trophy.

Captain Joe smiled but didn't take it from her. "That wouldn't be Harry Summerling's antique spyglass, would it?" He plopped a white captain's hat on his head and began tying the front of the boat to a cleat on the dock.

"Yes!" Sai said. "I mean, probably? Mr. Summerling's the one who sent us to this island and set up all those puzzles, right?"

Captain Joe didn't respond. Or even glance up from the rope in his hands.

"We found it with a book about the history of secret codes and a letter from Mr. Summerling that said he was alive," Marly added, lowering the spyglass to her side. Captain Joe moved to the back of the boat and the kids walked along the dock beside him.

"Not to be rude or anything," Sai said. "But the letter also said you're supposed to give us something for the spyglass."

"Did you know Mr. Summerling was alive?" Stella asked.

"Do you know where he is?" Isla asked.

"Is he nearby? Can we see him before we go home?" Marly asked.

Captain Joe finished securing the boat, then reached for the spyglass. He tucked it into a tall, narrow pocket at the side of his pants. "Why don't you all come aboard?" he said, offering a hand. "We have some things to talk about."

They all gathered up their suitcases and

Marly's metal detector and hopped down onto the boat. It shifted in the water with each hop.

Captain Joe showed them where to stow their things and reminded them where the bathroom was. Marly took a quick peek down the stairs into the dark cabin below, wondering if Mr. Summerling was down there. She didn't see him.

Once Stella and the kids were settled on benches and chairs at the back of the boat, Captain Joe took off his hat. "First," he said, "I do indeed have some things for you." He went over to a cabinet, crouched down, and opened the door.

The kids grinned at each other, and Sai squeezed Marly's arm with anticipation.

The captain grabbed a basketball-size globe from the top shelf and gave it to Sai.

"Niiiice," he said as he held it in his lap and spun it with his finger.

"There's more," Captain Joe said. He pulled out a teddy bear, which he handed to Isla, and a walkie-talkie, which he handed to Marly.

"Oh! Thank you," Marly said. She and her old friend Aubrey used to talk to each other on walkie-talkies all the time. Unfortunately, Aubrey moved away at the beginning of the summer. And took the walkie-talkies with her.

Captain Joe had only given Marly one handset. "Is there another one of these?" she asked. "Or two?" It would be so fun to use walkie-talkies with both Isla and Sai.

Captain Joe gave her a curious look. "What do you think that is?" he asked.

"Uh . . . a walkie-talkie?" Marly said.

"No, it's a satellite phone," Captain Joe said.

Sai frowned. "What's a satellite phone?"

"It's a phone that gets its signal from a satellite above the earth rather than a cell tower," Captain Joe explained. "It allows you to get service in places where a cell phone doesn't work."

"Oh," Marly said, wondering what she needed a satellite phone for. She didn't even have a cell phone.

"Aw! Someone sewed Harry's name on the bear's foot. Isn't that cute?" Isla wiggled her teddy bear's floppy foot.

"There's one more thing in here," Captain

Joe said, stretching his arm deep inside the cabinet.

Marly glanced at the phone in her hand, the teddy bear in Isla's arms, and the globe in Sai's lap. "I bet we can guess what that last thing is," she said, suddenly making a connection.

Isla nodded knowingly.

"A daisy!" Sai exclaimed as Captain Joe emerged from the cabinet with a plastic daisy. He handed it to Stella.

She blushed. "Why, thank you," she said.

"So, what are we supposed to do with this stuff?" Sai asked, spinning the globe again.

Whenever Marly, Isla, and Sai had come upon a picture of a globe, a bear, a telephone, and a daisy, they knew they were nearing the end of one of Mr. Summerling's treasure hunts. They would "make a T" and stand on the spot where two imaginary lines drawn between the four pictures crossed. They always found something important beneath that spot.

But not this time.

They were done with Mr. Summerling's treasure hunts. Next week, Marly, Isla, and Sai would be starting fourth grade. And Stella would be back in her office doing whatever it was attorneys did.

"These are souvenirs, right?" Marly said. "To help us remember the fun summer we've had." Not that she would ever forget!

"Maybe," Captain Joe said with a twinkle in his eye. "But if you spend some time with each of these objects, you may find there's a little more to them than you first thought."

The kids looked at each other.

"What does that mean?" Isla asked.

Sai leaped to his feet. "It means we've got another treasure hunt!" he shouted.

Chapter 2

EVERYTHING WE NEED

"There can't be another treasure hunt," Stella said. "We're going home."

"Unless we're supposed to do the treasure hunt on the way," Marly said. They had a two-hour boat ride back to Seattle, then a three-hour flight home. That was plenty of time to solve some puzzles.

"Actually," Captain Joe said, rubbing the back of his neck. "Your flight has been canceled, so . . . you're not going home quite yet."

"What?" Stella cried.

Marly, Isla, and Sai gaped. *They weren't going home?*

"How do you know that?" Stella asked. "Do we have a new flight?"

"You'll have to call the airline," Captain Joe said. He put the hat back on his head. "And unfortunately, you can't do that from here. There's no cell service on this island."

"But you just gave me a satellite phone," Marly said, holding it up. "You said it would work where a cell phone wouldn't."

"Yes. If you know the number to call," Captain Joe said. "But you can't use it to access the internet."

Marly turned to Stella to see if she knew the number for the airline.

"It's in my email," Stella said.

"I can take you over to George Island," Captain Joe offered. "You'll have both internet and cell service there. But even when you do talk to the airline, I'm guessing you won't be able to get another flight until tomorrow."

"Tomorrow?" Stella said. She did not look at all pleased.

But Marly and her friends were thrilled. Another day on Summer Island. Maybe even another treasure hunt. That was wonderful news!

"Should we get our stuff and go back to the cabin?" Sai asked.

"Not yet," Stella said. "Let's get our flight squared away first. We also need to call your parents and let them know the change of plans."

"Don't worry, Stella," Isla said. "Our parents will understand."

"Yeah, it's not your fault our flight was canceled," Sai said.

Stella winced. "Please take us to George Island," she said to Captain Joe. "Once we know when our new flight is, we can figure out what to do next."

Captain Joe nodded. "It'll take us about forty-five minutes to get there." He opened another cabinet and took out some life jackets. "Put these on and we'll be on our way." He passed them around, then went to untie the boat.

"By the way," he said as the boat drifted away from the dock. "If you'd like to see Harry today, you should know that you currently have everything you need to do that."

"You know where Harry is?" Stella asked.

"No," the captain said, not quite meeting her gaze. "He moves around a lot. But as I just said, you have everything you need to find him. And now, because your flight was canceled, you also have the time." He tipped his hat to them, then went inside the wheelhouse and started the boat.

Stella let out a big breath of air and sat

back in her seat. But Marly, Isla, and Sai were growing even more excited as they turned everything Captain Joe said over in their heads.

"So, not only do we have another treasure hunt," Sai said, "it sounds like this time Mr. Summerling is the treasure!"

"Captain Joe said we have everything we need to find Mr. Summerling," Isla said as they roared across the open water, their hair blowing across their faces. "What do we have?"

"A globe," Sai said, tapping on it with the palm of his hand. "A teddy bear, a phone, and a daisy."

"We also have a spyglass," Marly said. "Maybe." They'd given it to Captain Joe. Was it still in his pocket?

"I don't know," Isla said. "I think our first clue is in the stuff Captain Joe gave us rather than the thing we gave him." She hugged the bear to her chest.

Isla is probably right, Marly thought. She turned the phone around in her hand. "Maybe we're supposed to call him on this," she said.

"We don't have a number," Isla pointed out.

"I think we have to make a T," Sai said, springing to his feet. He hopped over to the bench across from Marly and Isla, then gestured toward the seat to his left. "One of you go sit over there so you're across from Stella. Then we'll have our T. And where the lines cross, we'll find . . . something. Maybe a phone number for Mr. Summerling!"

"I doubt it," Marly said. But she got up and sat down across from Stella anyway. "Right now, the T is there." She pointed to a spot in the middle of their square seating area. "If we go sit at the front of the boat, our T would be up there. We could make a T anywhere."

"Marly's right," Isla said. "I don't think we're supposed to make a T this time."

"But we always make a T," Sai argued. He strode over to the cabinet where Captain Joe had gotten the four objects. "Unless the T is in there?" He opened the door and pulled out a couple more life jackets, a fishing net, and some rope. Marly and Isla wandered over as he tried to pry up the bottom shelf.

Stella turned. "I don't know if you should be taking things out of that cabinet," she said. "This isn't our boat."

The shelf didn't budge anyway.

"I don't think there's anything we need in here," Isla said. She helped Sai shove everything back inside the cabinet.

Marly went to sit beside Stella. She stared at the plastic daisy in Stella's hand. "Hey, I

wonder why you got a fake daisy instead of a real one," she said.

"I'm allergic to daisies," Stella said as she absently spun the daisy one direction, then the other. "Most flowers, actually. Harry knew that."

"You're allergic to

flowers and I'm allergic to bees," Isla said, dropping into the seat next to Marly.

Isla had actually gotten stung by a bee on Summer Island. It was one of the scariest things Marly had ever seen. And plunging an EpiPen into Isla's leg was one of the scariest things she'd ever done. But she'd done it. And now Isla was just fine.

Sai plopped down across from Marly, Isla, and Stella, and for the next few minutes, they sat in companionable silence. Then Sai leaned curiously toward Stella. "What is that?" he asked.

"What is what?" Stella asked.

But Marly saw what Sai meant. "It looks like there's a paper or something taped around the stem of your daisy," she told Stella. Why would there be a paper wrapped around that daisy stem?

Chapter 3

STUMPED!

Stella picked at the tape with her fingernail and unwound a long narrow strip of green construction paper from the stem of her daisy.

"It's another code," Marly squealed with delight as Stella stretched the paper out in front of them. It read:

uudscy tf tysl zj guszuc ahv jnfgcrqz

"Can I see?" Sai asked. Stella passed it over,

and Sai stared at it with deep concentration.

"Careful it doesn't blow away," Isla said. The boat was moving pretty fast now. Wind blew their hair all around their faces.

"I'll get our notebook so we can write it down," Marly said, leaping up. She went over to the cabinet where they'd stowed their things and grabbed the notebook and a pen from her bag. It was the same notebook they'd been using all summer to work out Mr. Summerling's puzzles.

Marly sat back down next to Stella and opened the notebook to a clean page. There weren't many of those left. Sai read the letters off to her, and Marly copied them down.

"Well," Stella said as she stood up and stretched, "I know I'm not supposed to help with the puzzles, so I think I'm going to get out of the wind for a bit."

"Okay," Isla said.

Stella headed for the wheelhouse, and Sai slid into her seat. The kids continued to study the puzzle.

"I'm stumped," Isla said finally. "Do either of you have any ideas?"

"Not yet," Marly said, biting her lip. But they'd solved all the other puzzles. There was no reason to think they wouldn't solve this one, too.

"Is it another one of those—what did you call it?" Sai asked. "The thing where you shift all the letters in the alphabet one, two, or more positions?"

"You mean a Caesar cipher?" Isla said, holding her hair in her fist. "I don't think so. Look at this first word. It starts with two *U*s. Can you think of a single word in the English language that begins with two of the same letters?"

"We saw some weird words that began with two *A*s in the Scrabble dictionary," Marly reminded everyone. That was when they were solving the treasure hunt inside Mr. Summerling's house. Now, she flipped back to the page in the notebook where they'd written those words down.

"*A-A-H* and *A-A-L*," Isla read from the notebook. "I don't think that helps us at all."

"No, it really doesn't," Marly agreed. She turned back to the puzzle they were trying to solve.

"There are no vowels in either of the two-letter words." Sai pointed at the "tf" and the "zj" in their new puzzle. "So, we're not going to unscramble anything here."

"Plus, we've already had a Caesar cipher and a scrambled puzzle," Isla put in. "I don't think Mr. Summerling has ever repeated a puzzle in any of the treasure hunts."

"Good point," Marly said, chewing on the

end of her pen. But that didn't help them figure out this puzzle, either.

"How many different secret codes are there, anyway?" Sai asked in a tired voice. "A million?"

Marly patted the side of her head. "Why didn't we think of that before?" She hopped to her feet.

"Think of what before?" Sai asked.

"The book we found with the spyglass and letter," Marly said, running back to the cabinet where they'd stowed their things. She unzipped the front pocket of her suitcase and pulled out *The History of Secret Codes*. She'd forgotten how thick it was. More than three hundred pages.

Marly brought the book back to her friends. "All of the codes we've seen so far are in here," she said as she scanned the table of contents. "Morse code, the Caesar cipher, pigpen, even the one we used to find the cabin when we

got to Summer Island. Remember how we
wrapped that long strip of paper around the
stick that Captain Joe gave us? That's called
a—" She paused while she tried to figure out
how to pronounce the word. " 'Scytale'?"

"This is another long strip of paper," Sai
said, holding it up. "Maybe we have to find
something to wrap it around?"

Marly shook her head. "We've already had
that code."

"Also, there are spaces between the words in this puzzle," Isla added. "There weren't with the other puzzle."

Sai scratched his nose. "Well, let's go through that book and see if there's a code we haven't already solved that looks like this one."

It's as good of a strategy as any, Marly thought. She paged through the book, searching for a code that looked similar.

They would figure this out. Marly was sure of it.

But soon, the boat began to slow down. "We're almost to George Island," Captain Joe called from the wheelhouse.

Marly's head popped up. They were heading into a cove with a huge marina. This island had a totally different feel than the quiet, tree-covered Summer Island. Besides all the boats in the marina, the entire hillside was lined with houses and shops, and there were a lot of people milling around.

"We haven't solved the code yet," Sai said as Stella strolled back to them.

"You've got time," Stella said, folding her arms. "Though I am hoping we'll still be able to get home today."

And Marly and her friends were hoping to solve not only this puzzle, but the entire treasure hunt!

"If we go home today, we may not be able to see Mr. Summerling," Isla said.

"That's true," Stella admitted.

"Don't you want to see Mr. Summerling?" Sai asked.

"Don't you have a million questions for him like we do?" Marly asked.

Stella perched on the seat across from them. "Of course I do," she said. "But it's more important that we get you three home."

Marly strongly disagreed. Getting answers to their questions felt far more important than going home.

"Maybe we'll be able to talk to him on the phone," Stella said, patting Marly's knee. "Or maybe you'll solve that puzzle and learn that Mr. Summerling is waiting for us back in Sandford."

It was true they had no idea where Mr. Summerling was. He could be back home. But Captain Joe said they had everything they needed to find him, *and* they had the time. That made Marly think he was somewhere around here, not back home.

They had to solve this puzzle. And they had to do it before they headed for the airport.

Chapter 4

DROPS OF PAINT

"Look at that! Four bars," Stella said happily as she held up her cell phone. She moved to the front of the boat to check her email and make her phone call.

Captain Joe secured the boat to the dock, then turned to the Treasure Troop. "I'm going to take a walk up that hill and grab a cup of coffee. Would you like to come with me and see a little of George Island?"

Marly glanced over her shoulder at the quaint little town. "No, thanks. We've got a puzzle to solve," she said. Isla and Sai nodded in agreement.

"Suit yourselves," Captain Joe said. He put one foot up on the edge of the boat and hoisted himself onto the dock.

Marly, Isla, and Sai returned to their notebook with fresh resolve.

uudscy tf tysl zj guszuc ahv jnfgcrqz

What could it mean?

Marly picked up the strip of paper they'd found wrapped around Stella's plastic daisy. Had she missed something when she copied the puzzle into their notebook?

Isla took a turn paging through the code book. And Sai picked up the globe and spun it again, lightly touching his finger to the sphere to slow it down. "Hey," he said when it stopped spinning, "there are little silver blobs of paint on this globe."

Marly and Isla looked over.

"And they're not random blobs, either," Sai went on. "Each one is covering a letter on one of the country names. There are—" He slowly turned the globe while he counted. "Nine of them!"

"Huh," Isla said, sitting up a little straighter. "I agree. That doesn't look random at all."

Is this another puzzle? Marly turned a page in her notebook. "What letters are covered up?"

"The *P* in People's Republic of China," Isla said. "The *O* in Singapore, the *B* in Brazil."

Marly wrote them all on a new sheet of paper while Isla and Sai slowly turned the globe, scanning for more silver dots.

"There's also an *N*, a *G*, an *E*, and—" Sai frowned. "I don't know what letter is covered up here because I don't know what country that is. Do you?" He showed it to Isla, pointing to a country in Africa.

"Not sure," she said. "It could be *L* if the country is Angola. It could be *R* if it's Angora."

"Angola is a country in Africa," Stella said as she returned to them with her cell phone in hand.

Marly added an *L* to her list of letters.

"The captain was right. We're not going home until tomorrow morning," Stella said with a heavy sigh. "Our flight is at ten o'clock."

For Stella's sake, Marly tried to hold her excitement in. Sai, on the other hand, jumped up, raised his fist in the air, and shouted, "Hooray!" But he quickly lowered his arm when he saw the expression on Stella's face.

"At least we have the whole day to work on the treasure hunt," Isla said. She turned to Stella. "We found a new puzzle. On the globe!"

"Well, before you go any further, I'd like you to call your parents," Stella said. "You can let them know we'll be home around three tomorrow afternoon." She held out her phone.

Marly didn't really want to take time to do that right now. Not when they had two puzzles to solve. But she knew they should.

"Fine. I'll go first," Sai said, taking the phone.

Stella rubbed her arms. "While you're

doing that, I'm going to go get some sunscreen," she said. "If any of your parents want to talk to me, let me know."

Sai punched in a number, then put Stella's phone to his ear. "Hi, Mom," he said cheerfully. "Guess what?" He told her about the change in flight plans, the puzzles they'd been working on, and the fact that Mr. Summerling was alive! He answered a few questions with "Yes," "No," and "I don't know," finally ending with, "Okay, I will. Bye." Then he passed the phone to Isla.

Her conversation was similar to Sai's until she said, "Of course I've got my EpiPens." She didn't mention getting stung by the bee and needing to use one of those EpiPens on this trip, but Marly thought that was probably for the best. That was a story Isla could tell her mom in person.

Then it was Marly's turn. But when she called home, she got her mom's voice mail.

"Uh . . . hi," she said. "This is Marly. I'm calling to tell you our flight got canceled, so we won't be home until tomorrow afternoon. Also, Mr. Summerling is alive and we're

going to find him! Don't worry. We're all fine. And I'm wearing my eye patch. See you tomorrow. Bye."

She felt kind of grown-up all of a sudden. Being away from home with her friends instead of her family, managing her eye patch and changes in plans. She was taking care of herself.

"All done?" Stella asked as she returned to the kids.

"Yep," Marly said. She gave Stella the phone, and Stella gave her a tube of sunscreen in return.

"I want you all to use that," Stella said.

"Okay," Marly said, opening the cap.

"So, what did the code that was wrapped around my daisy say?" Stella asked.

"Oh, we didn't solve that one yet," Sai said. "We found these dots on the globe and we realized that was another puzzle. So, we decided to work on that one instead." Sai showed her the globe.

"Interesting," Stella said, gazing down at it.

Marly finished with the sunscreen and passed it to Isla. Then she picked up her notebook and sat back down. "Did we find all the dots?" she asked.

"I'm not sure," Isla said. She leaned over and slowly turned the globe.

"Use the sunscreen, honey," Stella said as she gently touched Isla's knee.

Isla grudgingly took the sunscreen, squeezed a blob into her hand, then passed the tube to Sai. Once everyone was properly protected from the sun, they returned to the puzzle.

"I don't think we got this *E*." Sai pointed to New Zealand on the globe.

"And there's an *O* we missed," Isla said.

Marly added them to the other letters in their notebook. "Is that it?" she asked after a couple minutes of silence.

"I think so," Isla said, biting her lip. "So what do we have?"

"*P, O, B, N, G, E, L, E,* and *O*," Marly read from her notebook. "We could've found them in any order, so maybe we have to unscramble the letters and make words."

"We've already had a code like that," Sai pointed out.

"True," Isla said. "But I'm not sure what else to try." She stared at the letters. "I see the word *GLEE*."

"And *POGO*," Marly said. She wrote them both down.

"And *GOOP*," Sai put in. "And *GLOBE*!"

"Globe?" Marly said. That couldn't be a coincidence!

Marly crossed out the *G, L, O, B,* and one of the *E*s in the notebook so they could see which letters were left.

P, O, N, and *E.*

Could she make any words with those letters? "*PEON*?" she said. "Is that a word?"

"How about *OPEN*?" Isla said. "Globe open?"

"Or . . . open globe!" Sai said.

Chapter 5

UNBREAKABLE!

"I've got doughnuts and croissants," Captain Joe announced as he approached the boat with a large white box.

Stella reached for the box, but Captain Joe shook his head. "I've got it," he said. The boat rocked as he jumped down. He set the box on a table and everyone crowded around.

"Thank you for this," Stella said, helping herself to a croissant with almonds.

"Yeah, thanks," Marly said. She and Isla each grabbed chocolate doughnuts.

Sai stared hungrily into the open box. "Can we have both a doughnut and a croissant?" he asked.

"Sure! There's plenty." Captain Joe ruffled Sai's hair, then turned to Stella. "Did you get ahold of the airline?"

"Yes. Our new flight is tomorrow at ten o'clock," she said as the kids took a break from their puzzle to enjoy their treats. "I assume we'll spend another night on Summer Island?"

"Uh . . ." For some reason, Captain Joe looked a little uncomfortable with the question. "I don't think I can answer that yet."

"Because it depends on whether we find Mr. Summerling today, right?" Marly guessed.

"I can't answer that," Captain Joe repeated. He tipped his face to the sky. "But the sun is shining. It's a beautiful day. Since we have no place else to be right now, I think we'll just

stay right here for a while."

The kids stopped chewing.
There was something about
the way Captain Joe said
"we'll just stay right here
for a while" that made
Marly suspicious. *Would
they find the next clue here on George Island?*

"In fact, maybe I'll catch a short nap in the
front of the boat," Captain Joe went on. "You
all are welcome to stay here or go into town.
There are a couple of nice museums."

"Uh . . . ," Marly said.

"That sounds fun, but . . . ," Isla said.

"We've got a treasure hunt to solve!" Sai
said as he popped the last bite of croissant
into his mouth.

Captain Joe turned to Stella. "How about
you? Would you like to visit one of the
museums?"

"Oh, I don't know," Stella said, running a

hand through her hair.

"We don't mind," Marly said.

"I think they'll be a while," Captain Joe told Stella. "You can put your contact info in my phone, and I'll give you a call when we're ready to move on." He pulled his cell phone from his front pocket and offered it to her.

Aha! Marly thought. *Sounds like we're staying right here until we solve these puzzles.* She wondered how long that would take.

"Well, I would enjoy walking around town," Stella gave in. She entered her info into Captain Joe's phone, grabbed her purse, and waved goodbye. Captain Joe moved to the front of the boat. And the kids returned to the globe.

"So, how do we open this?" Sai asked. "Is there a latch or something?"

Marly didn't see one.

"Try twisting it," Isla suggested.

Sai put one hand on the North Pole and the other hand on the South Pole and turned his

hands in opposite directions. "It's working . . .
I think," he said, gritting his teeth. But the
two halves obviously didn't turn easily.

"Careful you don't drop it," Marly said. She
put her hands out beneath the globe, ready to
catch it if it fell.

Sai braced the bottom of the globe against
his thigh and held it in place while he twisted
some more. "There we go," he said as the top
finally came off.

Inside the globe was a folded-up sheet of
paper. Isla grabbed it and unfolded it while
Sai laid the two globe halves on the seat
beside him.

Isla's eyes grew wide. "Whoa," she said.

Marly leaned over. " 'Whoa' is right," she
said, blinking a couple of times. It made her
dizzy to look at that code.

"That's not a code," Sai said with a scowl.
"That's just the alphabet repeated over and
over again."

"Wait, I saw something like that in that book we found," Isla said. She laid the paper in Marly's lap and reached for the book. "I don't remember what the code was called, but I remember seeing it. At first, I thought it was a word search, but—" She thumbed through a bunch of pages, then stopped. "Here!" She held the book so Marly and Sai could see.

"That's it!" Marly said.

"The Vi-Vig—how do you say that?" Sai asked.

Isla took a stab at it. " 'Vigenère cipher'?" she said. She scanned the first paragraph.

47

"It was invented in the year 1586, and it says here it's an unbreakable code!"

"If it's unbreakable, how are we supposed to break it?" Sai asked.

Isla kept reading. "The paper we found in the globe isn't actually the code," she said. "It's the table we'll use to *crack* the code. We need a message to be decoded, a keyword, and this table to figure out the message. That's how a Vigenère cipher works."

"So, what's the keyword?" Marly asked.

"And where's the message we have to decode?" Sai asked. "It's like the book says—impossible!" He stamped his foot.

"Nothing is impossible," Marly said. "Not

where the Treasure Troop is concerned." She picked up their notebook, but she wasn't sure what to do with it yet. If that paper was just a table they needed for reference, did she really need to copy it into the notebook?

"I wonder if the code we found wrapped around Stella's daisy is the message we need to decode," Isla said.

"Oh, maybe," Marly said. "We may not have to make a T with the things Captain Joe gave us, but I bet they all still fit together somehow." She turned back to the page in their notebook where she'd copied the code from the daisy:

uudscy tf tysl zj guszuc ahv jnfgcrqz

"Maybe it's all one big code that leads us to Mr. Summerling," Sai said loudly in the direction of Captain Joe. "Is that right, Captain Joe?"

But the captain lay sprawled out across a bench, his cap covering his face. It appeared as though he was sound asleep.

"It's okay," Marly assured Sai. "We'll figure this out. We found the Vigenère table inside the globe. We found the message to decode wrapped around the daisy. So, the keyword is probably either on the phone or on the teddy bear."

"Maybe it's in a voice mail message," Sai suggested.

Marly picked up the phone. "Do satellite phones have voice mail?" she asked. If so, how would they access it?

"Or . . . ," Isla said, reaching for the teddy bear. She held it so Marly and Sai could see the stitching on its foot. "Maybe the keyword is *Harry*."

Chapter 6

PUTTING IT ALL TOGETHER

"O kay, so how do we do this Vigenère code?" Sai asked.

"Looks like there are a couple of steps to it," Marly said, glancing back and forth between the code from the daisy and the book in Isla's lap.

Isla flipped her hair over her shoulder. "Let's start by writing *HARRY* over and over again right above the message we found wrapped around Stella's flower."

Marly put an *H* above the first *U*, an *A*

above the second *U*, an *R* above the *D*, another *R* above the *S*, and a *Y* above the *C*. "Like this?" She turned the notebook toward Isla.

"Yes. But keep going," Isla encouraged. "Don't worry about spaces between words. Just keep writing *HARRY*, *HARRY*, *HARRY* until you've got a letter above every letter in that message."

While Marly followed Isla's instructions, Sai put the globe back together and set it on the table beside him.

When Marly finished, she had:

harryh ar ryha rr yharry har ryharryh
uudscy tf tysl zj guszuc ahv jnfgcrqz

"Now we need the Vigenère table," Isla said.

They had two copies of that: the one on the paper they found inside the globe and the one in the book.

"I don't want to write in the book," Isla said.

"Where's the paper copy?"

It was under the notebook on Marly's lap. She pulled it out and handed it to Isla.

"The *U-U-D-S-C-Y* line is our message to be decoded." Isla pointed at it in the notebook. "And the *HARRY*, *HARRY*, *HARRY* is our keyword line. Can I borrow your pen?"

Marly gave Isla her pen, and Isla wrote *MESSAGE* above the top line of the Vigenère table, then turned the paper sideways and wrote *KEYWORD* to the left of the table going down.

"That's so we don't forget which is which," Isla said, handing the pen back to Marly. "Now we go letter by letter. The first letter from the keyword line is an *H*." She ran her finger down the left column of letters on the table until she came to the *H*. "And *H* goes with *U*, so we follow the *H* line all the way across to the *U*." She slid her finger over. "Then up to the top, and that'll tell us what the first letter of the

	A	B	C	D	E	F	G	H	I	J	K	L	M	N	O	P	Q	R	S	T	U	V	W	X	Y	Z
A	A	B	C	D	E	F	G	H	I	J	K	L	M	N	O	P	Q	R	S	T	U	V	W	X	Y	Z
B	B	C	D	E	F	G	H	I	J	K	L	M	N	O	P	Q	R	S	T	U	V	W	X	Y	Z	A
C	C	D	E	F	G	H	I	J	K	L	M	N	O	P	Q	R	S	T	U	V	W	X	Y	Z	A	B
D	D	E	F	G	H	I	J	K	L	M	N	O	P	Q	R	S	T	U	V	W	X	Y	Z	A	B	C
E	E	F	G	H	I	J	K	L	M	N	O	P	Q	R	S	T	U	V	W	X	Y	Z	A	B	C	D
F	F	G	H	I	J	K	L	M	N	O	P	Q	R	S	T	U	V	W	X	Y	Z	A	B	C	D	E
G	G	H	I	J	K	L	M	N	O	P	Q	R	S	T	U	V	W	X	Y	Z	A	B	C	D	E	F
H	H	I	J	K	L	M	N	O	P	Q	R	S	T	U	V	W	X	Y	Z	A	B	C	D	E	F	G
I	I	J	K	L	M	N	O	P	Q	R	S	T	U	V	W	X	Y	Z	A	B	C	D	E	F	G	H
J	J	K	L	M	N	O	P	Q	R	S	T	U	V	W	X	Y	Z	A	B	C	D	E	F	G	H	I
K	K	L	M	N	O	P	Q	R	S	T	U	V	W	X	Y	Z	A	B	C	D	E	F	G	H	I	J
L	L	M	N	O	P	Q	R	S	T	U	V	W	X	Y	Z	A	B	C	D	E	F	G	H	I	J	K
M	M	N	O	P	Q	R	S	T	U	V	W	X	Y	Z	A	B	C	D	E	F	G	H	I	J	K	L
N	N	O	P	Q	R	S	T	U	V	W	X	Y	Z	A	B	C	D	E	F	G	H	I	J	K	L	M
O	O	P	Q	R	S	T	U	V	W	X	Y	Z	A	B	C	D	E	F	G	H	I	J	K	L	M	N
P	P	Q	R	S	T	U	V	W	X	Y	Z	A	B	C	D	E	F	G	H	I	J	K	L	M	N	O
Q	Q	R	S	T	U	V	W	X	Y	Z	A	B	C	D	E	F	G	H	I	J	K	L	M	N	O	P
R	R	S	T	U	V	W	X	Y	Z	A	B	C	D	E	F	G	H	I	J	K	L	M	N	O	P	Q
S	S	T	U	V	W	X	Y	Z	A	B	C	D	E	F	G	H	I	J	K	L	M	N	O	P	Q	R
T	T	U	V	W	X	Y	Z	A	B	C	D	E	F	G	H	I	J	K	L	M	N	O	P	Q	R	S
U	U	V	W	X	Y	Z	A	B	C	D	E	F	G	H	I	J	K	L	M	N	O	P	Q	R	S	T
V	V	W	X	Y	Z	A	B	C	D	E	F	G	H	I	J	K	L	M	N	O	P	Q	R	S	T	U
W	W	X	Y	Z	A	B	C	D	E	F	G	H	I	J	K	L	M	N	O	P	Q	R	S	T	U	V
X	X	Y	Z	A	B	C	D	E	F	G	H	I	J	K	L	M	N	O	P	Q	R	S	T	U	V	W
Y	Y	Z	A	B	C	D	E	F	G	H	I	J	K	L	M	N	O	P	Q	R	S	T	U	V	W	X
Z	Z	A	B	C	D	E	F	G	H	I	J	K	L	M	N	O	P	Q	R	S	T	U	V	W	X	Y

KEYWORD

message is. See? It's an *N*!" She nudged Marly. "So, start a third line below the *U-U-D-S-C-Y* and put *N* below the *U*."

"Huh?" Sai said, wrinkling his nose. "I don't get it."

Marly didn't, either.

"Okay, let's do the next letter," Isla said.

"We always start with the keyword line of the message. That's the *HARRY, HARRY, HARRY*. The second letter is *A*." Isla put her finger on the A in the keyword line of the Vigenère table. "That goes with the second *U* on the message line." She slid her finger along the entire row of letters until she got to *U*. Then she matched it with the letter above, which also happened to be a *U*. "*A* and *U* equal *U*," she said.

"Oh! I think I get it now," Marly said as she put a *U* beside the *N* in her notebook. Isla was so smart!

"Can I try the next one?" Sai asked.

"Sure." Isla handed him the Vigenère table. He peered at the notebook in Marly's lap. "The third letter on the keyword line is *R*," he said. "So, we go down to the *R* line, then over to—" He glanced at the notebook again. "*D!* Then up to the top, which is *M*."

"*N* . . . *U* . . . *M*," Marly said as she wrote *M* in the notebook.

"Did you want to take a turn, Marly?" Sai asked.

It was nice of him to offer, but Marly shook her head. That table really bugged her eyes. "You two take turns," she said. "I'll tell you what letters are next and then you can tell me what each letter translates to."

"Sounds good," Isla said as she took the table back from Sai.

It was a good system. Fifteen minutes later, they had the entire message decoded:

NUMBER TO CALL IS INSIDE THE SPYGLASS

"Yes!" Marly pumped her fist in the air. "So, all these objects, including the spyglass, really *do* fit together." They would use the telephone to call Mr. Summerling. And hopefully they would get to see him, too!

"Okay, but where's the spyglass?" Sai asked.

"Captain Joe has it," Marly said.

They hurried to the front of the boat, where Captain Joe was still sound asleep. His chest rose and fell with every snore.

The kids glanced hesitantly at each other.

"Should we wake him?" Isla asked.

"Of course we should," Sai said. And without waiting for Marly to weigh in on that, he cleared his throat. "Ahem. AHEM!"

The captain stopped snoring for a second, but with the hat over his face, it was hard to tell whether he was actually awake.

"Um, excuse me?" Isla said politely. "Captain Joe? Are you awake?"

The captain removed his hat from his face and blinked at Isla. "I am now," he said. "Nothing like a little catnap in the morning sun." He yawned and stretched and slowly sat up. "What's going on?"

"Could we please see that spyglass again?" Marly asked. She showed the captain her notebook. "See? We solved the code, even though it's an impossible code. And the message says the number to call is inside the spyglass."

"Inside the spyglass, huh?" Captain Joe rose to his feet. "I put it in a drawer to keep it safe. Let's go see what we can find."

The kids followed him into the wheelhouse and over to a cabinet of drawers beneath a map on the wall. He opened the bottom drawer and pulled out the spyglass.

He twisted and turned the long tube, and a minute later, the spyglass was in two pieces. There was a small paper wedged inside one of the halves. Marly pulled it out, unfolded it, and read it out loud: "360-555-0189."

"That sounds like a phone number,"

Captain Joe said. "But it's not a number I've ever used to get ahold of Harry."

"Well, let's try now," Sai said.

Captain Joe reached for his cell phone.

"No," Marly said. "I think we should use the phone you gave us!" She hurried over to where she'd left it, pressed the power button, and entered the number. Then she listened.

"Hold it so we can all hear," Sai said eagerly.

Marly held the phone in her outstretched hand, but all they heard was a series of long, slow beeps.

Chapter 7

ANOTHER ISLAND

"What's going on?" Stella asked as she returned to the boat.

"We solved the codes!" Sai replied.

"Both of them," Isla added.

"There was a phone number hidden inside the spyglass," Marly explained. "We're pretty sure it's how we're supposed to get ahold of Mr. Summerling, but we tried the number and all we got was a lot of beeping."

"Maybe there's something wrong with that phone," Sai said. "Can we try a cell phone?

We've got service here, right?"

Captain Joe reached into his pocket and pulled out his phone. "What's the number again?" he asked.

Isla read it off and the captain punched it in. But the result was the same: a series of long, slow beeps.

"Wait, don't hang up!" Isla tipped her ear toward the phone. "There's something about that beeping . . ."

Everyone got quiet and listened. Some of the beeps were long, some were short.

Sai let out a low groan. "It's another code, isn't it?" he said, slumping into a chair.

Short-short . . . long-short . . . long-short-short.

"Is it Morse code?" Marly asked. She remembered when Sai had gotten separated from her and Isla in Mr. Summerling's house a couple weeks ago, he'd used Morse code to let them know where he was.

Sai shrugged. "I don't know," he said. "I only know *S-O-S* in Morse code."

Marly turned to Captain Joe. He pressed his lips together and looked everywhere except at the kids. Which only convinced Marly she was right. "It *is* Morse code, isn't it?" she said with a grin.

But before Captain Joe could answer, the beeping stopped and there was a strange scratching sound on the phone.

"What's that?" Isla asked.

The scratching stopped, and the beeping began again: long-short-long-short . . .

"That sounded like a cassette tape being rewound," Stella replied.

"What's a cassette tape?" Sai asked.

Stella and Captain Joe exchanged looks.

"There was a time not too long ago when people had answering machines instead of voice mail," Stella spoke over the beeping. "And messages were sometimes stored on a cassette tape that could be rewound, erased, and used again." The beeping stopped and the scratching sound returned. Stella pointed at the phone. "That's what it sounded like when an answering machine tape rewound."

The beeping began again. Long-short-long-short . . . long-long-long . . . long-long . . . short. A longer pause. Then short-short-long-short . . . short-short . . . long-short . . . long-short-short.

"That's pretty slow for Morse code," Captain Joe said, rubbing his chin.

"Maybe it's slow so we have time to write it down," Isla said.

"That could be why we keep hearing that scratching sound, too," Sai said. "If the message is on repeat, we have to know when it begins." He elbowed Marly. "Get ready to copy the message when it starts over."

"On it," Marly said, opening their notebook to a new page. She made a dot for every short beep and a dash for every long beep she heard.

Sai watched over her shoulder. "What are the up-and-down lines?" he asked.

"Shh!" Marly hissed. She couldn't listen to her friends and to the message at the same time. Captain Joe said it was slow for Morse code, but it was fast if you were trying to write it all down.

"The up-and-down lines are the longer pauses," Marly explained when the beeping stopped and the scratching began. "They're probably spaces between words." She held her notebook so everyone could see what she'd written:

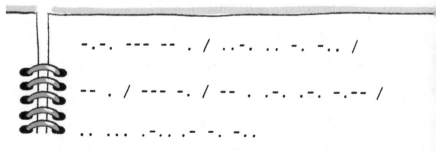

-.-. --- -- . / ..-. .. -. -.. /

-- . / --- -. / -- . .-. .-. -.-- /

.. ... .-.. .- -. -..

"Do you know Morse code?" Sai asked Captain Joe. "Do you know what that says?"

The captain ended the call and tucked his cell phone back inside his pocket. "I do, but I think Harry would want you three to figure it out on your own."

"Aww," Sai said. "How are we supposed to do that?"

"I'll go get that history of secret codes book," Isla said, dashing off. When she returned a few seconds later she said, "Guess what? There's a whole chapter on Morse code in here. And there's even a chart." She turned the book so everyone could see it.

Good thing we have that book, Marly thought.

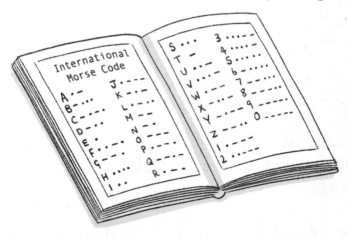

"Well, let's get translating," Sai said. "Long, short, long, short." He read the first letter in their notebook.

"That's a *C*," Isla said, and Marly wrote it down.

"Long, long, long. That's *O*!" Sai said. "I know that one from *S-O-S*!"

They kept going and a few minutes later, they had the entire message decoded:

COME FIND ME ON MERRY ISLAND

"Is that where Mr. Summerling is?" Sai asked. "On Merry Island?"

"Maybe," Marly said. "Where's Merry Island?"

They turned toward Captain Joe.

"There's a map right here." The captain gestured toward a map on the wall.

Marly, Isla, Sai, and Stella went to check it out. It showed all the islands in the area.

"Here's where we are now." Captain Joe touched the map and everyone moved in for a closer look.

"There it is! Merry Island." Sai pointed it out.

"Huh." Captain Joe squinted. "I don't think I've ever been to that island."

"Will it take long to get there?" Stella asked.

"Probably thirty to forty minutes," Captain Joe said. "I'll go untie the boat."

Marly, Isla, and Sai tightened their life jackets, then moved to the front of the boat, where they had a better view.

"We're getting closer to finding Mr. Summerling," Sai said, rubbing his hands together.

Isla's eyes shone with excitement. "I can't believe we're really going to see him again!"

The captain cut the motor, and Sai turned around in his seat. "Is that it?" he called. "Is that Merry Island?"

"Yep," the captain called back.

Marly slid her patch to the side so she could get a better look at the island. It was smaller than George Island. Smaller than Summer Island, too. A tall wooden fence seemed to surround the whole island, but she couldn't see anything beyond it.

Captain Joe steered toward a long dock. There was a small yellow building at the other end of the dock. A sign above the door said Welcome to Merry Island.

An older woman stepped out of the yellow building and strolled up the dock. Her gray hair hung in a long braid over her right shoulder. She waved to them as they approached.

"Rebecca?" Captain Joe said as he brought the boat right up against the dock with a light bump. "Is that you?"

"You know her?" Sai asked.

"Hello, Joe." The woman smiled, revealing a gap between her two front teeth. She held out her hand, and Captain Joe tossed her one of the ropes.

"I probably shouldn't be surprised to find you here, should I?" Joe said, and the woman smiled again.

"Who do we have here?" the woman asked as she tied the rope to a cleat on the dock.

Joe went to tie up the other end of the boat. "This is Stella Lovelace, Marly Deaver, Isla Thomson, and Sai Gupta." They each waved when the captain said their name. "They're all friends of Harry's."

The woman nodded. "And I'm Rebecca Walker," she said as the kids clambered out of the boat.

"Are you a friend of Harry's, too?" Stella asked Rebecca.

"You might say that," she said mysteriously.

"Where is he?" Marly asked, glancing around.

Sai elbowed her. "The message said to come find him," he said. "So, let's do that. Let's go find Mr. Summerling!" He charged down the dock toward the yellow building.

"Wait for us!" Marly called as she and Isla hurried after him.

"Hold on!" Rebecca called. "No one goes ashore until they give me the password."

Chapter 8

THE PASSWORD IS . . .

Marly, Isla, and Sai stopped in their tracks.

"'Password?'" Marly turned around slowly. They'd solved several puzzles this morning, but they hadn't come across any password. Unless a password and a keyword were the same.

"Is the password *Harry*?" Isla asked as they walked back toward the boat.

"No," Rebecca said.

"How about *Summerling*?" Marly tried.

"No." Rebecca shook her head.

"How about *globe, bear, telephone,* or *daisy*?" Sai said. "Or *spyglass*?"

Rebecca laughed. "You're guessing. You need to *find* the password, not guess the password."

"How are we supposed to find it?" Sai threw his hands in the air. "You said we're not allowed to go ashore."

"You're welcome anywhere on the dock," Rebecca said.

The kids locked eyes. *Does that mean the password is somewhere on the dock?*

"And if you're hungry, there are sandwiches and soft drinks in the caboose," Rebecca added.

"Caboose?" Sai repeated.

Rebecca waved her hand in the direction of the yellow building. "That's what we call that building over there. It was once an actual train caboose."

Sai looked over curiously. "Well, I'm hungry," he said. "Let's go check it out!"

The kids trooped down the dock, but Stella and Captain Joe remained on the boat. Marly paused at the door to the caboose. "Aren't you coming?" she called to the adults.

"I think we're going to enjoy the sun for a while," the captain replied as Rebecca climbed into the boat.

"You go ahead." Stella waved at them. Then the adults started chatting like old friends.

"That's weird," Marly said, crossing her arms.

"Yeah, what are they talking about?" Isla asked.

"Who cares? Let's eat, and then let's figure out the password so we can find Mr. Summerling," Sai said.

He opened the door and they all stepped inside the caboose. There was another door right across from them. Marly walked over, hoping to get a better look at the island. But there was nothing to see except the tall wooden fence.

A small sandy beach separated the dock from the fence. Though when Marly took a closer look, she noticed a door in the fence. It was easy to miss because it blended in.

Marly turned around. There was a small round table with a single chair tucked into a corner and a counter with three stools off to her right.

Isla climbed onto one of the stools while Sai walked around behind the counter, pulled premade sandwiches and cans of soda from the refrigerator, and set them on the counter.

Marly grabbed a sandwich but did not sit down. Neither did Sai. They both wandered around, glancing up and down the plain wood walls, searching for clues.

"I don't see anything that could be a password. Do you?" Sai asked.

"No," Marly said. She took a bite of her sandwich. Ham and cheese! Yum!

Isla hopped down from her stool and inspected the underside of the counter. "Me neither," she said.

They finished their sandwiches and Marly said, "Let's check out the dock."

They wandered slowly up and down the entire length of the dock. They studied every single board.

Nothing.

"You're not giving up, are you?" Captain Joe called to the Treasure Troop.

"Of course not," Marly called back. Though it might have seemed like it to the adults, because she and Isla and Sai were just standing around now. But they weren't sure what to try next.

"I understand you've got everything you need to find the password," Rebecca said.

"How does she know what we have?" Sai asked the others in a low voice.

"We don't have anything," Marly said, holding out her empty hands. They didn't even have their notebook right this second. It was on the boat. Along with the book about codes, the globe, the phone, the bear, and the daisy. Did they need any of that?

"Hey, Treasure Troop!" Stella stood up and waved. "That sun is pretty bright. Why don't you come get some more sunscreen?"

Marly's arms did feel warm. "I'll go get it,"

she said. She climbed down into the boat and saw that the adults were now gathered around the table playing some sort of card game.

"It's in the front pocket of my suitcase," Stella told Marly. "Go help yourself."

Marly went to the cabinet where they'd stowed their things. She found Stella's bag, unzipped the front pocket, and pulled out a tube. Oops, that was aloe, not sunscreen. She shoved it back inside the pocket and pulled out another tube. Sunscreen! But as she started to close the cabinet, her metal detector caught her eye.

Hmm . . . would that be useful right now? she wondered. Their notebook and the book about codes probably would be. She grabbed them and stuffed them into her bag. She dropped the sunscreen in there, too. *It couldn't hurt to bring the metal detector*, she decided. She grabbed it along with her bag

77

and climbed back onto the dock.

"Really? You brought the metal detector?" Isla's right eyebrow shot up.

Marly shrugged. "Why not? We've tried everything else."

They all slathered on more sunscreen, then Marly turned on the metal detector. A low hum came from the machine.

Together, they strolled slowly up the dock again, the metal detector guiding the way in front of them. Four boards before

they reached the end of the dock, the metal detector's hum suddenly became a loud, high-pitched shriek. Just for a second. Then the low hum returned.

Marly backed up and the metal detector shrieked again. The ear-piercing sound didn't stop until Marly swung the machine away from that board.

"There's something under there," Sai said, dropping to his knees.

"You mean besides water?" Isla said.

Sai peered between two boards. "Maybe what we want is underwater?"

"I don't know." Isla crouched down next to Sai. "The water's pretty deep." She wiggled the board in front of her. "Hey, this board is loose!"

"Is it?" Marly said. She turned off the metal detector and laid it on the dock behind her. Then she bent down and helped Isla and Sai pull on the board until it came all the way up.

"See anything?" Sai peered into the water.

"Not really," Isla said, clutching the board.

All Marly saw were plants swaying underwater. If the password was hidden in something down there, she wasn't sure how they would ever get to it.

Then Isla turned the board over, and a slow smile spread across her lips. "Look!"

There was a metal plate on the underside of the board.

"That must be what made the metal detector go off," Sai said.

"There's something etched into it," Marly said.

They put their heads together and saw:

Chapter 9

FOLLOW THE PATH

"**I**s that the password?" Sai asked.

"I think it's another code," Marly said. She opened her notebook and wrote it down.

"He, two, spsad?" Isla tried to break the message into words, but she didn't get very far.

"What kind of code has both letters and numbers?" Sai asked as he rested on the heels of his feet.

A seagull squawked overhead. In the distance, large and small boats roared across the open water.

Isla twisted her hair as she studied the notebook. "Wait, I remember a code like this. I saw it in that book."

"Did you read that whole book straight through or something?" Sai asked. "How do you remember all these codes?"

Isla blushed. "I have looked at it a lot. It's interesting!"

"Well, I brought it if we want to look at it again now," Marly said, reaching into her bag.

Isla waved her away. "I don't think we need it," she said. "Not unless I'm wrong. In the code I remember, the numbers tell you how many letters are in each word. Then you have to unscramble each word to read the message."

"Okay, let's see if that works," Marly said. The code read:

HETWOSPSADRSIETERESUHO38245

The first number was a 3, so Marly counted off three letters with her pencil and drew a line between the *T* and the *W*. Then eight more letters and another line between the *R* and the *S*. Two letters and a line between the *I* and the *E*.

"You could be right, Isla," Marly said with growing anticipation. "If you unscramble *S-I* you've got *IS*."

"*IS* is a word!" Sai exclaimed. "One, two, three, four." He counted out loud. "The next line goes between the *R* and the *E*. And then we have five letters left."

When she was done, Marly's page looked like this:

HET|WOSPSADR|SI|ETER|ESUHO 38245

"Well, that's easy," Marly said. "The first word is *THE*. The third word is *IS*."

"Fourth word is *TREE*!" Sai put his finger over the *E-T-E-R*.

That helped Marly figure out the last word. "*HOUSE*," she said.

Isla laughed. "And guess what the second word is. *PASSWORD!*"

"The password is *tree house*?" Sai said with a scowl. "We could've guessed that."

"Yeah, but we didn't," Marly said.

"But we found it," Isla said, raising both hands for high fives.

Marly and Sai slapped high fives with Isla, then they all scrambled to their feet and raced to the boat.

"We know the password! We know the password!" Sai announced.

The adults glanced up from their game as Marly, Isla, and Sai skidded to a stop beside them on the dock.

"It's *tree house*," Marly said, holding the notebook so the adults could see it.

Rebecca smiled. "That's exactly right." She pulled a key from her front pocket, then handed it up to Isla. "Now, if you walk through the caboose and across the sand—"

she pointed, "you'll come to a door."

"I saw it!" Marly said excitedly.

"This key will unlock that door," Rebecca said.

Stella started to stand up, but Rebecca motioned for her to sit back down. "Sorry. The Treasure Troop must go on alone from here," she said.

Stella didn't look happy about that. "But we won't even be able to see them," she said. "I'm responsible for them. As Harry's attorney—"

Rebecca squeezed Stella's shoulder. "And because you're Harry's attorney, I'm asking that you wait a bit. Please."

The kids all looked at each other. What did *that* mean?

"Don't worry. They'll be fine," Rebecca assured Stella. "As long as they stay on the path. You'll do that, won't you?" she asked Marly, Isla, and Sai. "You'll stay on the path?"

Isla and Marly nodded.

"Well . . . that depends," Sai said. "I mean, if we're being chased by a wild boar or something—"

Rebecca laughed. "I assure you, there are no wild boars on Merry Island."

"So, where are we going?" Marly asked. "Where does the path lead?"

"You'll know when you get there," Rebecca replied.

"I bet it leads to Mr. Summerling," Sai said in a soft singsong voice.

Probably, Marly thought. *But then why do we have to go alone?*

"Now off to your adventure." Rebecca waved them toward shore.

They all took off their life jackets and tossed them in the boat.

"Let's go!" Sai said, leading the way.

"Oh! I almost forgot," Rebecca called as they approached the caboose. "Remember who you are. That will always get you through!"

"Where have we heard that before?" Isla asked.

Marly remembered. It was in the second letter they'd received from Stella, the one that started them on the treasure hunt inside Mr. Summerling's house.

"We're friends!" Sai raised his fist in the air. *FRIENDS* was the code word that had gotten them inside Mr. Summerling's house.

"Good friends," Marly said, wrapping one arm around Isla and the other around Sai.

"Best friends." Isla draped an arm around Marly. And together they marched through the caboose, then jumped down onto the sand.

When they reached the door in the fence, Isla inserted the key. The handle turned easily, and the door opened, revealing thick woods. Just like behind Marly and Mr. Summerling's houses. Just like on Summer Island.

"What is it with Mr. Summerling and woods?" Sai asked.

"Good question," Marly said as she stared

into the dark forest. Then she turned to her friends and reached for their hands. "Ready?"

"Ready," Isla said. They all stepped forward together, and the door swung closed behind them.

The path wasn't wide enough for them to walk side by side, so Sai charged ahead, followed by Marly, then Isla. A breeze rippled through the trees.

"How much farther?" Sai asked as he swiped at bugs that swarmed around them.

Marly brushed a stray cobweb from her face. "It's not that big of an island, so it can't be too far," she said.

"I bet we'll come to another door at the end of this path and we'll have to type in *F-R-I-E-N-D-S*," Sai said. "And *that's* where we'll find Mr. Summerling. The End!"

"Are you ready for it to be the end?" Marly asked.

"Yes," Sai said right away. Then he thought

about it for a second. "Well . . ."

"Are you?" Marly asked Isla over her shoulder.

"I'm not sure," Isla admitted. "I want to find Mr. Summerling. But it's been such a fun summer. It's sad that it's almost over."

Marly felt the same way. She remembered how lonely she was when Aubrey moved away, and the summer had stretched endlessly in front of her. But she'd made new friends. Acquired a tree house. Solved lots of puzzles. And taken this awesome trip.

"I'm so glad Mr. Summerling brought us together," Marly said with a smile. "It's been a great summer!"

Isla nodded and smiled back.

"Hey, the summer isn't over," Sai said as they came to another fence. This one was even taller than the other one and it was covered in vines.

"Neither is this treasure hunt," Isla

said. The path ended at a black metal door.
There was no doorknob. No keypad like at
Mr. Summerling's house.

But beside the door was a touchscreen that
was embedded into the fence. Sai walked
right up to it. "Uh . . . I don't think we're going
to enter *F-R-I-E-N-D-S* into that," he said.

There were no letters on the touchscreen.
Just a 0, a 1, and an Enter key.

"How does this door even open without a doorknob?" Isla asked.

"No idea," Marly said, staring at it.

Obviously, they would have to figure out what to do with the touchscreen in order to open the door. And Sai was already on it.

"What are you doing?" Isla asked as Sai pressed the 1 button over and over again.

"Shh!" He counted on his fingers, then pressed the 1 button a few more times.

Marly raised an eyebrow at Isla, and Isla

returned a *"who knows, he might be on to something"* look in response. Finally, Sai touched the Enter button and stepped back expectantly.

The touchscreen buzzed loudly, startling them all.

"That wasn't right?" Sai sounded genuinely surprised.

"What wasn't right? What were you doing?" Marly asked.

"Well, we think the word we need to enter is *FRIENDS*, right?" Sai said. "But there are no letters to push, only numbers. So, I counted to *F*, which is the sixth letter in the alphabet, and then I pressed the 1 six times. And *R* is—I forgot what *R* is." He counted it out again. "The eighteenth letter. So, then I pressed the 1 eighteen more times and—"

"Did you only press the 1 button?" Isla interrupted.

"The 1 and the Enter," Sai said. "I pressed

Enter after I was done."

"But you never pressed 0?" Isla asked.

"No?" Sai said it like a question.

"Which means you really just pressed the 1 a hundred times," Marly said. Or however many times it took to count out all the letters in *FRIENDS*.

"I paused between each letter," Sai said.

"Maybe instead of pausing between each letter, we should try pressing the 0," Isla suggested.

"Okay," Sai said with a shrug. He pressed the 1 button six times for the *F* in *FRIENDS*, followed by the 0. Then the 1 button eighteen more times for the *R*, followed by the 0. Then nine 1s for the *I*, and 0. Five 1s for the *E*, and 0. Fourteen 1s, 0. Four 1s, 0. Nineteen 1s, 0, and finally the Enter button.

Bzzt!

Marly sighed. "That's not it, either," she said.

"Maybe we've got the wrong password," Sai

said as he leaned against the fence.

"What else could it be?" Marly asked.

"If it's a password we're looking for, maybe it's *TREE HOUSE*?" Isla suggested.

"We just gave that to Rebecca," Sai said.

"So? It's worth a try," Isla said. They counted out each of the letters in *TREE HOUSE* and tried that on the touchscreen.

Bzzt!

"I still think it's *FRIENDS*," Marly said. "Otherwise, why would Rebecca have said that about remembering who we are? It's the same exact wording we had for Mr. Summerling's house. We just have to figure out how to enter *FRIENDS* into this screen when all we have to work with is a 1, a 0, and an Enter button."

"You've got the code book in your bag, right?" Isla nudged Marly. "Maybe we should look for a code that's written in 1s and 0s?"

"And *only* 1s and 0s," Sai added.

Marly didn't know how to look that up in the index, so she started paging through the book. She went slowly enough to scan each page, but not so slowly she was actually reading. Until something caught her attention. A chart of 1s and 0s. She turned back a page to read the description.

"It's binary," she said triumphantly. "The language of computers."

"How does it work?" Sai asked.

Marly scanned the first few paragraphs. "It's like a switch," she explained. "It's either on or off, 1 or 0." She turned the page. "And look! Here's a chart of the alphabet in binary code."

"Two charts," Isla pointed out. "One for capital letters and one for small letters. Which one do we need?"

"I say we try them both," Sai said, returning to the touchscreen. "Tell me how to spell *FRIENDS* in binary."

"I'll start with the capital letters," Marly said.

A	01000001	N	01001110
B	01000010	O	01001111
C	01000011	P	01010000
D	01000100	Q	01010001
E	01000101	R	01010010
F	01000110	S	01010011
G	01000111	T	01010100
H	01001000	U	01010101
I	01001001	V	01010110
J	01001010	W	01010111
K	01001011	X	01011000
L	01001100	Y	01011001
M	01001101	Z	01011010

"01000110," Marly began. "01010010, 01001001, 01000101, 01001110, 01000100, and 01010011."

This time, a chime sounded, and the touchscreen went blank.

The kids waited, but nothing happened.

"Is the door open now?" Isla asked.

Sai pushed against it. "No," he said when it didn't budge.

"Maybe it slides open," Isla said. She looked for something to grip, but there was nothing.

"We heard a chime, not a buzz," Marly said. "And the buttons are gone. That has to be right!"

But how were they supposed to open the door?

"Maybe it's got a bug in it," Sai said. "You said it was a computer code."

"Ha! Maybe," Marly said.

"I thought you meant a real bug. Like these," Isla said, swatting at some insects.

Finally, the touchscreen crackled, and a picture filled the screen. A picture of—Marly squinted. Was that the inside of a motor home?

Then a familiar face came into view. "Well, hello there, Treasure Troop!" Mr. Summerling greeted them on the screen.

"Mr. Summerling! Mr. Summerling!" Isla exclaimed as they all crowded into the frame.

"You're alive!" Sai said. "I knew you were alive!"

"Can you hear us?" Marly asked.

Mr. Summerling chuckled. "Loud and clear. And I'm so happy to see you. So happy to see you together."

"He looks good," Isla said to Marly and Sai. And he did! He looked healthy and happy. And very much alive!

"Of course I look good," Mr. Summerling said. "I feel better than I've ever felt in my life!"

"Where are you?" Isla asked, pressing closer to the screen.

Mr. Summerling chuckled again. "I'm right inside. Would you like to come in?"

"Yes!" they all shouted at the same time.

"Then come on in," Mr. Summerling said, and the door in front of them clicked open.

Chapter 11

THE TRUTH ABOUT MR. SUMMERLING

Marly, Isla, and Sai stepped through the door and found themselves in a wide-open area about the size of the playground and soccer field at their school. There were a couple of motor homes and tents off to the side, near some scraggly bushes. And, right in front of them, a section of grass was roped off, and two people were crouched over squares of dirt with hand shovels and brushes.

"What's going on in here?" Isla asked.

"Are they digging for treasure?" Sai asked.

"You might say that," said a voice behind them.

They all whirled around and saw a man with white hair ambling toward them. Marly almost didn't recognize him because she'd never seen him in jeans and a T-shirt before. "Mr. Summerling!" she cried.

Marly and her friends raced toward him and threw their arms around him.

"It's so good to see you all," Mr. Summerling said as he hugged them all back.

"We did it!" Sai said. "We solved all the puzzles and we found you!"

"You sure did," Mr. Summerling said, hugging them all again. "And those weren't easy puzzles to solve."

"No, they weren't," Sai agreed.

Then the kids started talking all at once.

"Why did you want us to solve all those puzzles?"

"Yeah, why us?"

"Why'd you fake your own death?"

"Are you coming home?"

Mr. Summerling raised his hand like a stop sign to stop the questions.

"Sorry," Marly said. "But we have a lot of questions." And after all they'd been through, she thought they deserved answers to those questions.

"I know," Mr. Summerling said. He waved

to the people who were digging, and they waved back. "How about we go inside where we can talk?" He steered Marly, Isla, and Sai toward the largest motor home, and they climbed aboard.

"Whoa!" Sai said, wide-eyed. "Is this a camper or a house?"

Marly was wondering the same thing. There was a bedroom, a kitchen, a small sofa, a recliner, even a TV and fireplace. There was probably a bathroom somewhere, too.

"Is this where you've been living all summer?" Isla asked. She pulled the cat ears headband out of her hair, then repositioned it on her head.

"It would be so cool to live here," Marly said, turning a full circle.

Mr. Summerling gestured toward the sofa and one by one the kids sat down. "I've been here some of the time," he said as he lowered himself into the recliner. "I've also spent some time on Summer Island and on my boat—"

"Till that storm came up," Sai interrupted. "What happened? How did you survive the shipwreck?"

"Shipwreck? There was no shipwreck," Mr. Summerling said with a wry smile. "My fishing boat got loose in a storm late this spring. Floated way out into Canadian waters. But I was never on that boat. Not while it was loose. Imagine my surprise when someone found it and the coast guard declared me dead!" He tossed back his head and laughed. But he was the only one laughing.

"Everyone back home thinks you're dead, too," Marly said.

"I know," Mr. Summerling said in a more serious tone of voice. "But you know what?" He leaned toward them. "That's okay. People have always seen me as sort of a funny old man—"

"What? No! We don't," the kids started to protest.

"Please," Mr. Summerling raised his hand again. "We all know it's true. And if I'm being completely honest, I'd have to say I also rather enjoy being the subject of so much speculation. Let everyone back home wonder. Is Harry Summerling alive or dead? If they think I'm dead, that solves another of my problems."

Marly, Isla, and Sai exchanged confused looks. "What problem?" Isla asked.

"My son," Mr. Summerling said with a firm set to his jaw. "He's been trying to put me in an old folks' home and take control of my money for years. He doesn't like my spending it on treasure hunting and travel because he's afraid there won't be anything left for him. And there won't be if I can help it! It's my money. And my life. I'm not going back to Sandford. I'm staying here in the Pacific Northwest. I want to spend the rest of my days exploring, sailing, and hunting for treasure!"

"Is that what's going on over there?" Marly pointed toward the window where she could see the people digging in the dirt. "Are they hunting for treasure?"

"Yes," Mr. Summerling nodded. "A couple of archaeologists discovered evidence of an old colony on this island, so we've been searching for artifacts all summer."

"Artifacts or treasure?" Sai asked.

"Is there a difference?" Mr. Summerling asked.

Marly remembered how he always used to say not all treasure is silver and gold. And she, Isla, and Sai had certainly discovered that for themselves this summer. Sure, they'd found treasure. Not everyone would agree that a tree house and a trip to Summer Island was "treasure." But it was to them!

"Why did you set up all these treasure hunts for us?" Marly asked. It was still the main thing she wanted to know.

"Yeah, why *us*?" Sai asked. "You hardly know us."

"Oh, I know you better than you think I do," Mr. Summerling said. "I've been buying my newspaper at your family's store for years, Sai. I know you enjoy games, you sometimes struggle with school, and you're a little rambunctious from time to time, but you're also not afraid to take a risk."

Sai looked surprised. "That's all true!" he said.

"And Isla, you and I met two years ago when I became your senior buddy and we began writing letters back and forth,"

Mr. Summerling said. "I know you love a good puzzle and you're a little on the quiet side. Maybe even a little lonely. That's why you had so much time to write letters to an old man."

"Oh, I liked writing to you," Isla protested. "I also like getting mail!"

"I know," Mr. Summerling said. "And I'm glad you enjoyed our correspondence as much as I did. I've enjoyed watching you come out of your shell a bit as we've gotten to know each other. But I also had a feeling that the right friends your age could bring you out of your shell even more."

Isla blushed.

"And Marly." Mr. Summerling shifted in his seat. "We've lived next door to each other your whole life. I know how sad you were about your friend moving away."

Marly wasn't just sad when Aubrey moved away, she was devastated. It felt like the worst thing that had ever happened to her. But she'd learned to get along without Aubrey. She'd learned to stand on her own two feet. It didn't mean she and Aubrey weren't friends anymore, but their friendship had changed.

"I knew the three of you would be good for one another." Mr. Summerling brought his hands together. "But as busy as everyone is these days, I wasn't sure how you'd ever get to know each other. And you all live so close together, too. So," he winked. "I figured out a way for you all to spend some time together. By giving you a treasure hunt, or three, to solve."

"But how? How did you even set up those treasure hunts?" Isla leaned forward. "You were here. You didn't know everyone was going to think you died in that storm. How did you make us part of your will when even Stella Lovelace thought you were dead?"

"That's where my buddy Joe came in," Mr. Summerling explained. "He and I have been friends most of our lives. When the coast guard reported me missing, that gave me an idea. I sent Joe to Sandford with some papers for Stella and directions for setting up the treasure hunts. You'll remember that first letter Stella gave you didn't say for sure that I was dead. It said, 'If you are hearing this letter, I am missing, dead, or—'"

"'Abducted by aliens,'" Sai interrupted. "I remember that part!"

"Yes, well . . . ," Mr. Summerling looked rather pleased with himself, "I didn't know what was going to happen. I didn't know if you'd be able to solve the puzzles. If you'd find the tree house. If you'd find the tickets to Summer Island. If you'd even become friends. But I have to say everything has worked out so much better than I imagined. And now it's time to talk about the next step."

"The next step?" Marly said with a curious glance toward her friends. They looked equally intrigued.

"Yes," Mr. Summerling said, his eyes dancing with mystery and excitement. "It's about your final treasure, should you choose to accept it."

"Why wouldn't we accept it?" Sai asked.

"What is it?" Isla asked.

"Well, before we go any further, I think we should bring Stella Lovelace in on the conversation," Mr. Summerling said. "Is she here?"

"She's on the boat with Captain Joe and Rebecca," Sai said.

Mr. Summerling slowly rose to his feet. "Then let's go to the boat," he said. "I promise all of your questions will be answered."

Chapter 12

A NEW IDEA

Everyone on Captain Joe's boat was eager to hear about Mr. Summerling's final treasure. Marly, Isla, and Sai squeezed together on one of the benches, and Isla hugged the teddy bear in her lap. The globe, satellite phone, and plastic daisy remained on a table between Sai and Stella. Captain Joe stood behind them. And Mr. Summerling and Rebecca sat side by side, closer than they really needed to be.

Stella lifted an eyebrow at that. "Is there

something else you'd like to tell us?" she asked. She'd been as surprised as the kids to learn there'd been no shipwreck. But no one had quite figured out how Rebecca fit into the puzzle yet.

"Yes, I suppose so," Mr. Summerling said, putting an arm around Rebecca. "This lovely lady and I are getting married!"

"Oh, that's wonderful!" Stella clapped her hands and Mr. Summerling and Rebecca both beamed.

"Congratulations, friends," Captain Joe said, leaning over to shake their hands.

"Hooray!" the kids cheered.

"And we're going to sail around the world," Mr. Summerling said. His smile faded a bit. "Which is why we need to have this little meeting. I have a plan for my house. Or maybe I should say 'a wish.' Whether or not that wish comes true depends on the three of you." He fixed his eyes on Marly, Isla, and Sai.

"It does?" Sai said.

"Yes," Mr. Summerling said. "You've all been inside my house. I know you enjoy puzzles. Some will say this is a crazy idea, but . . . I'd like to turn my house into an escape room. Several escape rooms, perhaps. You've seen those, haven't you? People pay money to get locked in a room, and then they have to solve puzzles to get out."

"I've heard of those!" Isla said.

"I've been in one of those," Marly said. "Our whole family did one when we went on vacation last year."

"Lucky!" Sai said. "That sounds like fun!"

Mr. Summerling cleared his throat. "I'm glad that sounds like fun," he said. "Because I was wondering how you three might feel about running it!"

Marly's mouth fell open. "What?" she said.

"Us?" Isla said, equally shocked.

"For real?" Sai said.

Mr. Summerling nodded. "I would pay you, of course. I'm thinking we could start a college fund." He turned to Stella. "I assume you can draw up paperwork for all of this?"

Stella was obviously as surprised as the kids were. "Uh . . . yes, I can do that," she said. "But Harry, are you sure about this?"

"I've never been more certain of anything in my life," Mr. Summerling said, the smile returning to his face. "You know how I love puzzles and games. And so do these kids. I want to turn my house into an escape room, and I can't think of anybody I'd rather have run it than the three of them."

Marly didn't know what to say. Neither did Sai.

But Isla did. "Thank you, Mr. Summerling! That's amazing."

"So, you want to do this?" Mr. Summerling asked.

"Yes! We do! For sure!" They all spoke at once.

"Fantastic!" Mr. Summerling said. "You can take some of your favorite puzzles from this summer and use them in the escape room. That book you found on Summer Island should help, too. You can use several rooms. That might be fun. Make people solve puzzles to escape the whole house. Whatever you want. Just have a good time with it."

"We will," Sai promised.

"Good! I'm glad that's settled," Mr. Summerling said, patting his legs. "Because I've got a wedding to plan."

Everyone laughed. Rebecca grinned at Mr. Summerling, and he leaned over and kissed her on the cheek.

"I've got one more question," Marly said when the excitement died down. "Why was there a telephone, globe, bear, and daisy in all of our treasure hunts?"

"Yeah," Sai said, picking up the globe. "You never told us that."

"There must be a reason you chose *those* things, specifically," Isla said.

"Oh, there is," Mr. Summerling said. "They're representations of

117

the things I think are really important in life. Things that I hope you will find important, too."

"Huh?" Sai said. "I mean, I like globes and maps and GPSs, but I don't know how important they are."

"A globe represents the world," Mr. Summerling explained. "I think it's important to take time to explore the world."

Marly wanted to explore the world one day. The whole world! "How about the telephone?" she asked. "What's that for? To remind us to call people?"

"Yes, in a manner of speaking," Mr. Summerling said. "No matter where in the world you go, it's important to stay in touch with old friends. How about the bear? What do you think that represents?"

Everyone turned to Isla, who still held the bear on her lap.

"I don't know." She shrugged. "Bears . . . nature . . . wildlife?"

"I think it has something to do with books or the library," Sai said. "You used to work at the library. And there are a ton of books about bears. Not to mention the Little Bear statue outside." They'd solved one of their early puzzles there.

"The bear could also represent love or hugs," Marly said.

Isla looked confused.

"What?" Marly said. "It's a teddy bear! What do you do with a teddy bear? You hug it! You're hugging that bear right now."

"True," Isla said, blushing.

"Those are all good ideas," Stella said.

"So, what does the teddy bear stand for?" Captain Joe asked Mr. Summerling.

But Mr. Summerling didn't answer. "What do you think the daisy stands for?" he asked. He was clearly enjoying this.

"Love," Isla said right away.

This time Sai looked confused.

"Don't you remember?" Marly asked. " 'He loves me, he loves me not'?" Sai had never heard of that before the first treasure hunt.

"Oh yeah," he said now. "But the bear and flower can't both be love."

"I was thinking nature," Stella said. "But they can't both be nature, either."

"Are you going to tell us?" Marly asked Mr. Summerling.

"You know what?" Mr. Summerling said, rubbing his chin. "I don't think I am. These four objects all hold meaning for me. And maybe now they hold meaning for you, too. But that meaning doesn't have to be the same."

That made sense to Marly. And those objects certainly did hold meaning for her now. They were more than just a bear, a telephone, a daisy, and a globe. In fact, she wasn't sure she'd ever be able to think of those things separately, without thinking of the other three. In her mind, those four objects went together now. *Like the Treasure Troop!*

"I don't think it matters what each of those objects means by itself," Marly said. "But if you put them together, they mean friendship," Marly said. And friendship was the real treasure she, Isla, and Sai had uncovered. The only treasure that really mattered in the end.

ONE YEAR LATER

It was Preview Day for Summerling's Great Escape, and the line outside stretched past Marly's house.

"This is so exciting!" Isla squealed.

"I know!" Marly squealed back. It was almost as exciting as the day she got to stop wearing her eye patch for good. Her vision still wasn't as good as Isla's or Sai's, and it never would be. But it was better. Better than it would've been had she never worn a patch. She was glad now that she'd worn it most of the time when she was supposed to.

"Are all the rooms ready?" Marly's mom asked. Marly's mom had accepted Mr. Summerling's offer to serve as business manager for Summerling's Great Escape. They'd decided that Marly, Isla, and Sai would handle the puzzles, and Marly's mom would handle the money.

"The globe room is ready," Sai said.

"So is the teddy bear room," Isla said.

"And the telephone room," Marly's brother Nick said. Even he and his twin, Noah, had helped get Summerling's Great Escape ready.

"Don't forget the daisy room," Marly said.

"All right then," Stella Lovelace said, throwing open the front door. "Come on in!"

"Marly!" A girl with green hair rushed toward her and threw her arms around her.

"Aubrey!" Marly cried, hugging her back. "What are you doing here?" Aubrey had moved away a year ago.

"I'm back for a visit," Aubrey said. "Your mom told my mom about this, so I got here first because I wanted to be your first customer."

"Well, we're not really open yet," Sai said. "Today is a preview. People can walk through and see the rooms."

"And if they like what they see, they can

reserve a day and time," Isla said.

Hopefully, lots of people would come through today and make a reservation. Then Summerling's Great Escape would be off to a good start.

"Would you like a tour?" Marly asked, looping her arm around Aubrey's.

"Sure," Aubrey said. "But can we skip ahead to the secret passageway? I really want to see the secret passageway!" Her whole face lit up.

"You can't skip ahead," Sai said. "You have to do all the puzzles in order. Otherwise, you might not find the secret passageway."

Aubrey's face fell. "Oh," she said. "I'm not very good at puzzles."

"It's okay. We'll help you," Isla said, looping her arm around Aubrey's other arm.

"Of course we will," Sai said.

"What are friends for?" Marly said.

THE END